For Sadie, Emmett, Myrtle, and Asa

Henry Holt and Company,
Publishers since 1866
Henry Holt® is a registered trademark of
Macmillan Publishing Group, LLC
120 Broadway, New York, NY 10271
mackids.com

Copyright © 2020 by Deb Pilutti
All rights reserved.

Library of Congress Cataloging-in-Publication Data is available.
ISBN 978-1-62779-650-7

Our books may be purchased in bulk for promotional, educational, or business use.
Please contact your local bookseller or the Macmillan Corporate and
Premium Sales Department at (800) 221-7945 ext. 5442 or by email at
MacmillanSpecialMarkets@macmillan.com.

First edition, 2020
The illustrations for this book were created with gouache, PanPastel, and digital.
Printed in China by Hung Hing Off-set Printing Co. Ltd.,
Heshan City, Guangdong Province

1 3 5 7 9 10 8 6 4 2

Ten Steps to FLYING like a SUPERHERO

DeB PiLutti

Christy Ottaviano Books
Henry Holt and Company ☆ New York

Lava Boy and his favorite toy, Captain Magma, have saved the day many times.

Captain Magma knows he should be perfectly pleased with his superpowers.

His superstrength always comes in handy.

He can find lost toys using lava vision,

and his friendly personality has won over even the most evil of the supervillains.

Still, late at night, when the day's saving
is done, he dreams of flying.

He flew once—
it was thrilling.

But he hasn't been able to lure
a bird for another ride since.

What if Lava Boy sets him aside
for a newer, fancier superhero toy?
One who can fly.

It shouldn't be hard for a superhero
like Captain Magma to learn how to fly.
He just needs a plan . . .

STEP
NUMBER 1

Make a plan.
Lava Boy will help.

He is very smart
for a sidekick.

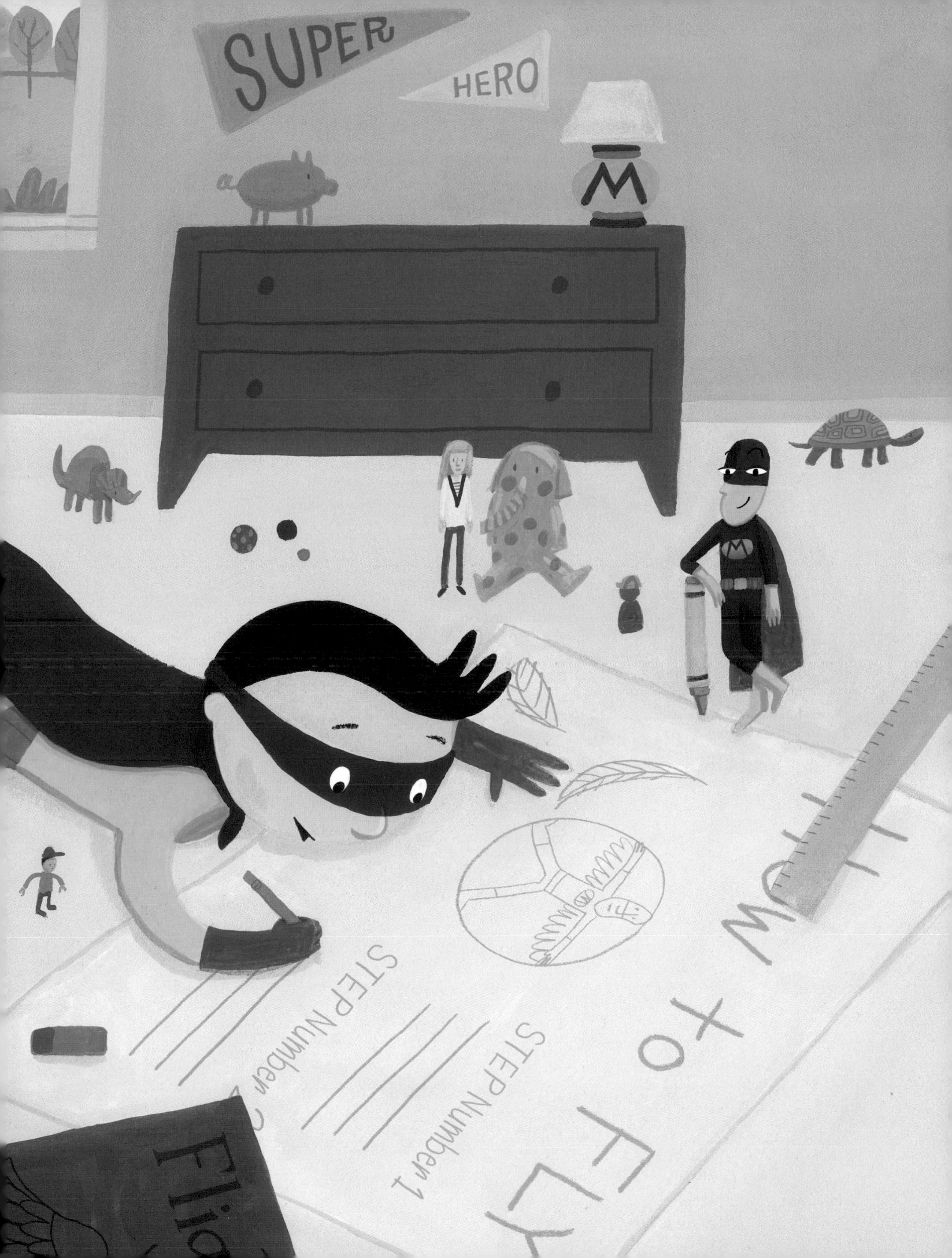
SUPER
HERO
HOW to FLY
STEP Number 1
STEP Number 2

STEP NUMBER 2

Gather the appropriate
materials:

scissors
glue
tape
paper
feathers
glitter
string
a parachute from
Skydiver Joe (he won't mind)

P.S. Don't skimp on the glitter.
There is no such thing as
too much glitter.

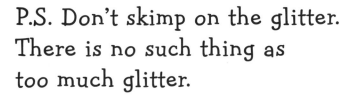

STEP NUMBER 4

Check your work.
Do the straps look like
they'll hold? Is there
enough glitter?

STEP NUMBER 5

Find a high spot for a launch.

It's important to consider safety at this point.

This is
NOT
a good →
IDEA.

Better.

STEP NUMBER 6

Don't look down.
Seriously.
Just look straight ahead
in the direction you
want to fly.

FLY!

Even if you are the tiniest bit scared.

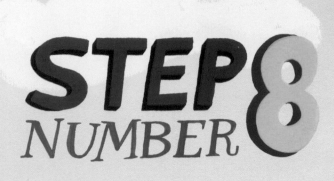

STEP NUMBER 8

Adjust course if necessary.

This is not always as easy as it sounds.

STEP NUMBER 9

Be prepared for anything.

You never know what kind of problem might arise.

STEP NUMBER 10

If you fail, pick yourself up,
make a new plan, and try again.

Tomorrow.